In My ROMANTASY Era

IN MY ROMANTASY ERA

Copyright © Octopus Publishing Group Limited, 2025

All rights reserved.

Text by Debbie Chapman

No part of this book may be reproduced by any means, nor transmitted, nor translated into a machine language, without the written permission of the publishers.

Condition of Sale
This book is sold subject to the condition that it shall not, by way of trade or otherwise, be lent, resold, hired out or otherwise circulated in any form of binding or cover other than that in which it is published and without a similar condition including this condition being imposed on the subsequent purchaser.

An Hachette UK Company
www.hachette.co.uk

Summersdale Publishers
Part of Octopus Publishing Group Limited
Carmelite House
50 Victoria Embankment
LONDON
EC4Y 0DZ
UK

This FSC® label means that materials and other controlled sources used for the product have been responsibly sourced

MIX
Paper | Supporting responsible forestry
FSC® C018236

www.summersdale.com

The authorized representative in the EEA is Hachette Ireland, 8 Castlecourt Centre, Dublin 15, D15 XTP3, Ireland (email: info@hbgi.ie)

Printed and bound in Poland

ISBN: 978-1-83799-931-6
eISBN: 978-1-83799-937-8

Substantial discounts on bulk quantities of Summersdale books are available to corporations, professional associations and other organizations. For details contact general enquiries: telephone: +44 (0) 1243 771107 or email: enquiries@summersdale.com.

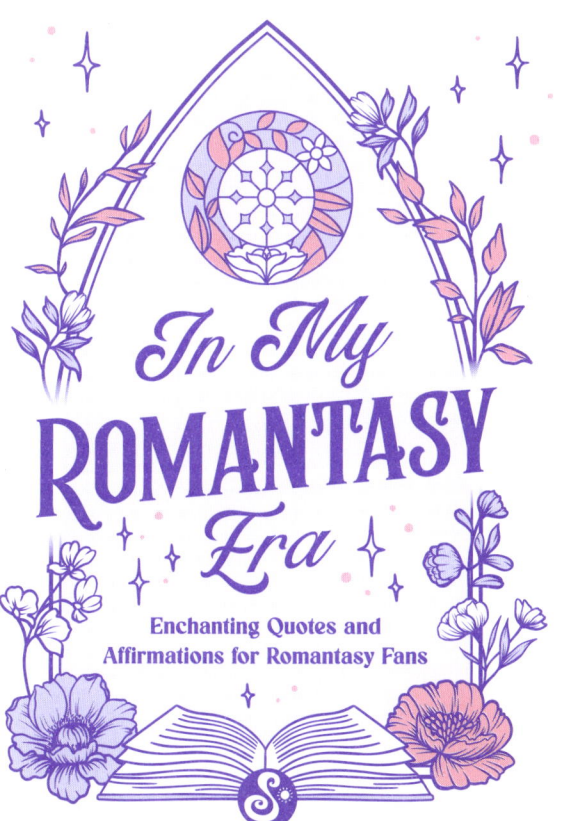

I'M JUST A GIRL, STANDING IN FRONT OF A ROMANTASY NOVEL, *asking it to destroy her emotionally*

The joys of book journalling

You may already track your reading, but embracing the apps and book journals that are available to you – or creating your own with a blank notebook – can really enhance your enjoyment of the books you've loved. It could be that you want to write full-blown reviews of each book, or you may prefer giving ratings to various elements of each read: what would you rate it out of five for immersion? For romance? For worldbuilding? For the chemistry between the characters? Or maybe you prefer a bingo-style tick list to track all the classic romantasy tropes. Forced proximity? Tick. A love triangle? Of course. Commoner-to-royalty? Bingo!

It's about the person who's holding your hand at the end. The person you can't let go of, no matter how hard you might have tried.

Helen Scheuerer,
Iron & Embers

Everyone is scared, princess. It is how we choose to use that fear that will define us. It is how we choose to use it that will determine the fate of our world.

Holly Renee,
A Kingdom of Blood and Betrayal

A BOOK A DAY KEEPS REALITY AWAY

I am the **SKY** and the power of every **STORM** that has ever been. I am **INFINITE**.

REBECCA YARROS,
FOURTH WING

Knowledge can only be wielded by those who dive into its depths and know the shape of it. Reading without true understanding is only wading in the shallows without a care for the monsters that lurk beneath.

ANDREA STEWART,
THE BONE SHARD DAUGHTER

You'd be brooding too if your soulmate kept trying to get himself killed heroically

A thousand plus **WORLDS** he has seen, yet when he **DREAMS**, he dreams of you.

AMBER V. NICOLE,
THE THRONE OF BROKEN GODS

She wasn't light; she was colour. Every single one, dancing otherworldly and bright over his unworthy eyes. She was the explosion of the vivid gleams and glows of the world around him, like a constant rainbow, shining not after the rain but during. She was everything he never deserved but longed for anyways.

HANNAH NICOLE MAEHRER, *APPRENTICE TO THE VILLAIN*

It took only a
HEARTBEAT
to fall for you

It looks like you are night incarnate, the stars in the sky, the power in my veins.

Gillian Eliza West, *Ruin*

He called to her the
way the forest did.
Called to something
deep and forgotten.
Something that longed
to come alive again.

Kristen Ciccarelli,
Edgewood

Dreaming of being swept away by my shadow daddy; stuck making spreadsheets

He kissed me as if I were air and he couldn't get enough. He kissed me like wildfire, consuming everything in its path. He kissed me as though I were the last drop of blood in the world, the only thing that could ever sate his hunger.

BRIAR BOLEYN,
ON WINGS OF BLOOD

"I LOVE YOU," HE WHISPERED, AND KISSED MY BROW.

"THORNS AND ALL."

SARAH J. MAAS,
A COURT OF THORNS AND ROSES

Romantasy book club

There are plenty of romantasy book clubs around including online ones that are super-accessible, no matter where you live. But if you want the joy of talking IRL about your favourite characters or geeking out about the latest instalment you have been dying to get your hands on, why not set up your own? It can be as simple as getting your friends to meet at a cozy café or pub once a month to discuss your latest reads. If you want to go more formal, you could advertise on a local forum or set up a group on social media to make new romantasy friends. Just make sure to have some questions prepared to help kick-start the conversation, and you'll all be talking about dragons and noble heroes and enchanted castles until the sun sets over the kingdom…

Opposites are not always in opposition; the day and night are equals. One isn't good and the other bad. But one does illuminate things while the other obscures, and that has to mean something too, I think.

HANNAH WHITTEN,
THE FOXGLOVE KING

YOU HAD ME AT
"we can't"

Some people call these guilty pleasure reads, but why should I feel guilt for wanting to escape to somewhere else, even for a little while?

Elizabeth Helen,
Bonded by Thorns

As long as
you are mine as
I am yours, we
have all the time
in the world.

Sue Lynn Tan,
Daughter of the Moon Goddess

MAY YOUR
DREAMS BE
AS SPICY AS
YOUR BOOKS

My favorite stories are the ones I can escape into. The ones where I can leave behind this bleak existence and be somebody else, even if just for a little while. Someone braver than me. Someone with the power to change their circumstances.

ANALEIGH SBRANA,
LORE OF THE WILDS

I BELIEVE THERE ARE FAR MORE POSSIBILITIES THAN HAPPILY EVER AFTER OR TRAGEDY.

EVERY STORY HAS THE POTENTIAL FOR INFINITE ENDINGS.

STEPHANIE GARBER,
ONCE UPON A BROKEN HEART

Create a cozy reading nook

Romantasy is all about immersion – epic feelings, sweeping landscapes, high stakes, slow-burn tension and shadowy fae and foes. What better way to sink into the world you love than by creating your very own reading nook? Key elements include somewhere comfy to sit or lie down, a reading light and space to display all your favourite books. Then add some fantasy elements such as fairy lights, swathes of fabric to form a dreamy canopy and some gorgeous curated wall art to set the mood. You can even buy bookish candles that smell like leather-bound tomes, sumptuous roses or dusty bookstores.

Emotionally damaged dragonrider energy only

This man could drag her down to hell and she'd gladly burn *for eternity.*

Kerri Maniscalco,
Throne of the Fallen

Came for the plot,
STAYED FOR THE SINGLE-BED SCENE

FOR ANYONE WHO HAS EVER BEEN TOLD THEIR SPARK SHOULDN'T BURN SO BRIGHT AND FOR ALL THE PEOPLE WHO LOVED THEM PRECISELY BECAUSE IT DID.

Penn Cole,
Spark of the Everflame

And then she smiles, bright and big like the night sky hanging above us. I fear she could rival the stars.

Lauren Roberts,
Reckless

Me, an intellectual: bonding with morally grey warlords in magical kingdoms

I love you like in the **STORYBOOKS.** I love you like in the **BALLADS.** I love you like a lightning **BOLT.**

HOLLY BLACK,
THE DARKEST PART OF THE FOREST

I don't think you realize how strong you are, because sometimes strength isn't swords and steel and fire, as we are so often made to believe. Sometimes it's found in quiet, gentle places.

REBECCA ROSS,
DIVINE RIVALS

Create your own fantasy

Why leave all the fun to the pros? If reading all about those lusty lovers and epic battles has got you feeling inspired, maybe it's time to turn your hand to writing your own story. Are you drawn more to a particular subgenre within romantasy? Maybe it's sword fights and honourable deeds that get your creative juices flowing. Perhaps it's the dragon-flight and descriptions of mythical mist-bound realms. Or perhaps it's the dirty bits – hey, there's no judgment here. Either way, all it takes is a blank piece of paper or your notes app, and off you go. You'll be creating worlds and letting your imagination run wild in no time.

> Her fingers felt small, yet substantial, when he wrapped his own around them. A jolt shot through him at the touch and she stopped, looking at him with a curious expression. Had she felt it, too?

NISHA J. TULI,
TRIAL OF THE SUN QUEEN

PLOT TWIST:
the repressed, angry demon is hot

Some wither within minutes, and others are carved forever into our souls.

Carissa Broadbent,
The Serpent and the Wings of Night

BUT I HAD NOT KNOWN THAT I WAS STRONG ENOUGH TO DO ANY OF THOSE THINGS UNTIL THEY WERE OVER AND I HAD DONE THEM.

I HAD TO DO THE WORK FIRST, NOT KNOWING.

NAOMI NOVIK,
SPINNING SILVER

YOU'RE A STORM I CAN'T OUTRUN

You are the fire of my **HEART**, and the beat of my drum. I am yours under **MOONLIGHT**. Until the rhythm **SINGS** no more.

SAARA EL-ARIFI,
FAEBOUND

If the story of your life were a book, I'd carry it with me across the world. I'd read it every night. And whenever I reached the ending of what had been shared with me, I'd open it to the first page and begin reading again.

DANIELLE L. JENSEN,
GILDED SERPENT

Let the fates decide

Add an element of magic and eliminate analysis paralysis by using tarot cards to choose your next read. You probably have a huge TBR pile and sometimes the problem is just picking which one to start next. Embrace the mystical and try your hand at divination by shuffling your tarot or oracle deck and taking the card that's calling to you. See if you can find any hints in the card that are telling you which book you should choose – or maybe it'll be blindingly obvious which one the fates have lined up for you. Perhaps there'll be a reason destiny has chosen this book – is there something in it that you need to learn, or reflect on?

Our souls were always meant to be one

I will love you today, tomorrow, and always. I will love you until the sun fades and the moon cracks and the stars burn away to husks. I will love you even after the world has forgotten our names and ground our bones to dust. You are my blood, my marrow, my heart. Not in a thousand lifetimes will I ever let you go.

LYRA SELENE,
A CROWN SO SILVER

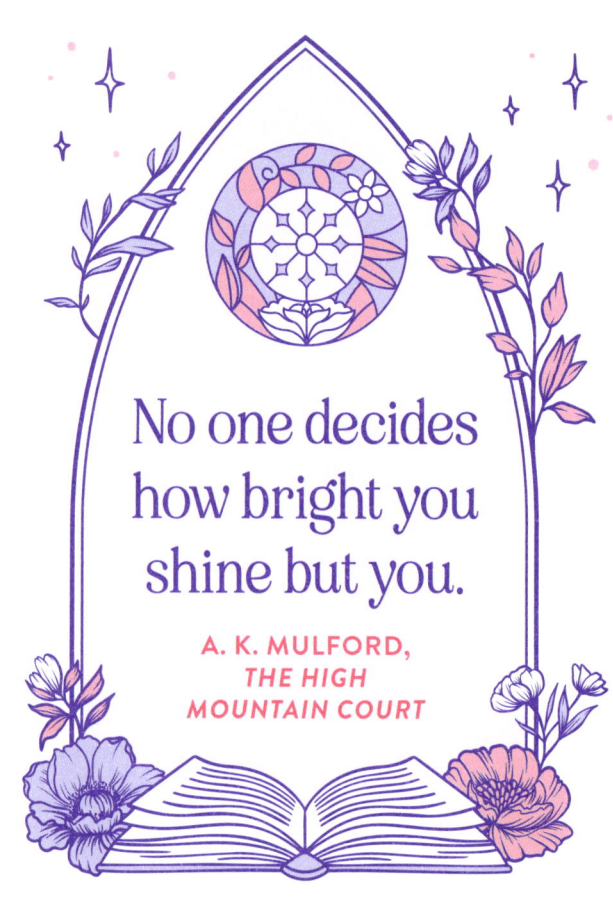

Not all **MONSTERS** *want to hurt you...*

She wanted to suspend time and live in the feelings he elicited in her, a warm, beautiful riot of colours in her dark heart.

Runyx,
Gothikana

Fear and bravery are often one and the same. It either makes you a warrior or a coward. The only difference is the person it resides inside.

Jennifer L. Armentrout, *From Blood and Ash*

In this house, we romanticize conflicted, dark antiheroes

YOU DON'T KNOW ANYTHING ABOUT WHAT IT'S LIKE TO FIND YOUR OTHER HALF.

I WOULD TAKE ANYTHING SHE CHOSE TO GIVE ME – THE TINIEST FRACTION OR HER ENTIRE WORLD.

ALI HAZELWOOD,
BRIDE

In another life, I would've tried to know her. I would've admired her and read her poems written by my own hand. I would've walked with her through fields of stardrops, danced with her in the stream.

CHARISSA WEAKS,
THE WITCH COLLECTOR

Savour the burn

Romantasy loves a simmer. These things can't be rushed – the glances, the tension, the one-horse scene, the battlefield declaration, the moment their fingers almost touch, the moment one of them says, "You belong to me." Relish the build-up – after all, this is the crown jewel of the whole genre. The slow burn may be agony, it may make you yell at the page, but it gives you time to believe in the love, rather than just swooning at it. See if you can spot every little foreshadowing, every small shift or lingering gaze, and you'll enjoy the moment when they finally kiss like the realm depends on it all the more.

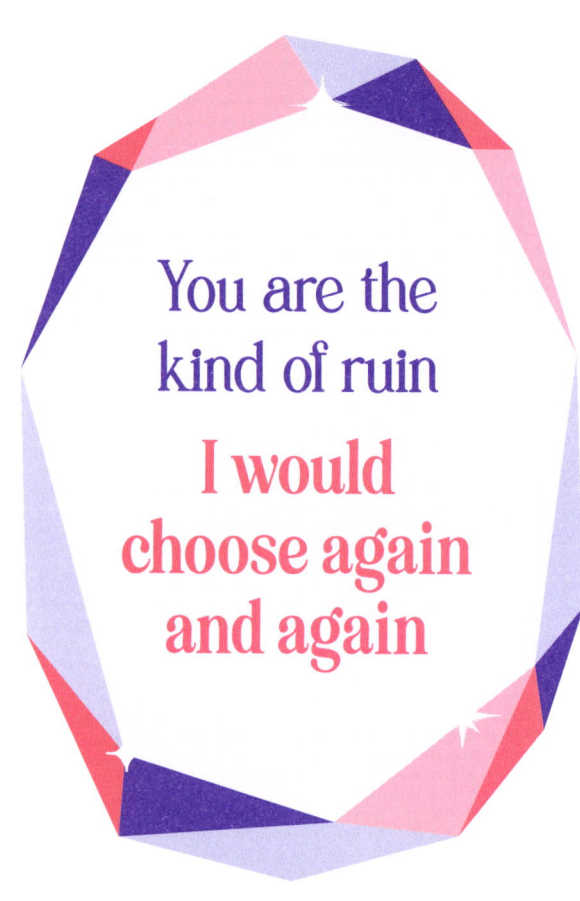

I knew we were
an inevitability —
as undeniable
as the crash of
thunder after
lightning
shatters the sky.

Geneva Lee,
Filthy Rich Fae

LET ME GUESS, YOU'RE ANOTHER

brooding immortal with a redemption arc

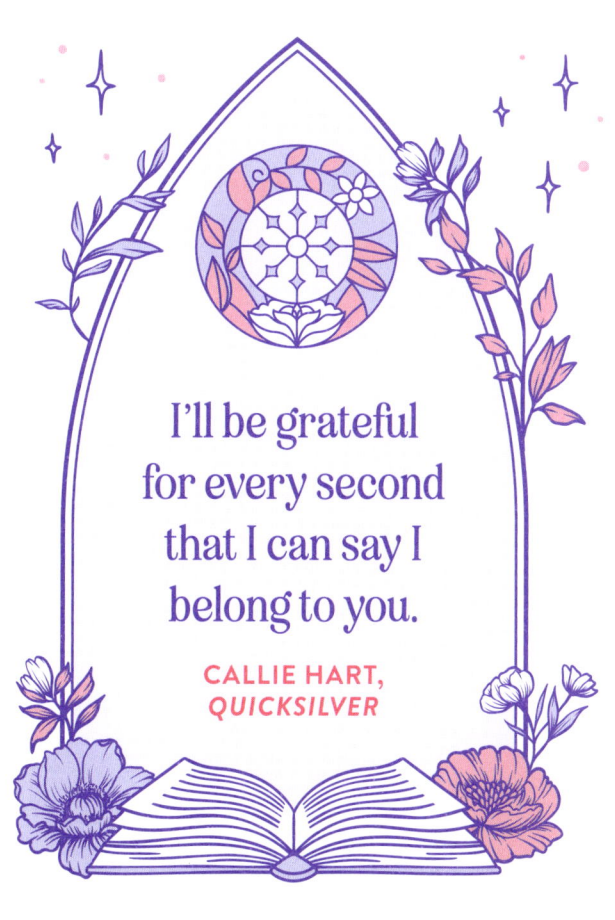

"I thought I lost you."
I breathe her in.
"Never," she whispers.
"Not until the sun casts its last ray and the moon bids the sky farewell."

Cecy Robson,
Bloodguard

The gods made you for me. Carved you from the stars themselves until I could no longer bear to gaze up at the sky without longing for you.

Holly Renee,
The Hunted Heir

He found himself no longer wanting to punish her for her faith in him. Instead, he found himself wanting to be worthy of it. He wanted to be the knight he had once been. Just for a moment.

HOLLY BLACK,
TITHE

GENUINE, IMPOSSIBLE AFFECTION BETWEEN TWO OPPOSING ENERGIES.

THE SUN AND THE MOON ORBITING EACH OTHER IN PERFECT SYNCHRONICITY.

S. T. GIBSON,
EVOCATION

Fan fiction

Fan fiction is popular for a reason: it allows you to take all your favourite parts of a book, and then play puppet-master with your favourite characters (or your least favourite, if you want to play *evil* puppet-master and finally see them get their comeuppance). Even if you don't fancy yourself as a writer, you can have a lot of fun coming up with imaginary storylines set in the world of your most beloved book – or books. What do you think is the backstory behind that wallflower fae? What happened after they kissed on the final page? What would happen if the High Lord from this book came upon the mysterious prisoner from that one – in the volcanic lair of your all-time favourite dragon?

Another day, another shirtless, damaged antihero to save

He smells of cool mountain air and sea breeze, of adventures taken and *adventures waiting.*

Berlyn Hayes,
Heirs of Secrets

It might not be easy to **FOLLOW** your own stars, but in the end, that's how we shine the **BRIGHTEST.**

ALEXIS CALDER,
KINGDOM OF BLOOD AND SALT

Magic, moods and MISTAKES

I'M TERRIFIED THAT ONE WRONG STEP WILL HAVE ME TIPPING RIGHT OVER THE EDGE, HEADFIRST INTO A FALL THAT I CAN'T RECOVER FROM.

Raven Kennedy,
Gild

What I know is that love is never a gift the Triada gives to break us. It is how he gives us wings. It is how he takes us to new heights, new depths. Love, real love makes us better.

Roseanna M. White, *Awakened*

10% logic, 90% romantasy tropes

This is **TENDERNESS.** And she is more afraid of it than anything else in their forsaken **KINGDOM.**

CHLOE GONG,
IMMORTAL LONGINGS

COME HELL OR HIGH WATER, I WILL GIFT YOU THE ENTIRE WORLD AND EVERYTHING IN IT.

EVERY DESIRE, HOPE AND WISH, TRAVELING UPON A SHOOTING STAR.

KRISTINA STANGL,
THE EMERALD PRINCE

Themed dinner party

Have fun planning a dinner party for your romantasy-loving friends (or for anyone at all – it's *your* party). You could come up with cocktails that suit the vibes of your favourite characters or pair your courses to different books; suggest a dress code based on your favourite series; design place cards for your guests with romantasy embellishments; dress the table in wine-red satins and deep-blue velvet runners; or even come up with a bookish quiz to play between courses. And, of course, the room should be practically *drowning* in fairy lights, moons and stars.

I love you. When everyone else is dust, I'll still love you. When the world itself runs its course and comes to an end, I will carry my love for you to the Hells and let it burn there with me for eternity.

MELISSA CARUSO,
THE IVORY TOMB

The kiss was an awakening. Like every kiss before ceased to exist. There was no moment before or after this. Here was eternity.

K. A. Linde,
The Wren in the Holly Library

To the ones who don't run with the popular crowd, the ones who get caught reading under their desks, the ones who feel like they never get invited, included or represented.

Rebecca Yarros, dedication in *Onyx Storm*

ENEMIES-TO-LOVERS, BUT MAKE IT FERAL

One was the sun and the other was the moon.

One was night and the other day.

But I had always been drawn to the night.

Always been awake and alive in the dark.

Always looked to the stars for answers.

J. A. JUDE,
STARGAZER

I WANTED HIM TO KISS
ME. I COULD ADMIT
IT TO MYSELF –

I WANTED HIS LIPS ON MINE
MORE THAN I WANTED
MY NEXT BREATH.

KATE GOLDEN,
A DAWN OF ONYX

Highlight the good stuff

There's a reason BookTokers love annotating their favourite books – and it's not just because it looks pretty. Highlighting (whether digitally or with highlighters, pens and sticky tabs) can help you easily come back to all the best spicy dialogue, killer insults, important character details, worldbuilding details and swoon-worthy descriptions. The act of annotating as you read can help deepen your emotional connection to and appreciation of the story, and you'll enjoy revisiting all your favourite parts that made the experience so special. Just make sure you find pens and highlighters that don't smudge the ink!

I'm not afraid of monsters – I'm emotionally entangled with one

Love can make
us do impossible,
beautiful, terrible
things. Love
can bloom
like revolution.

Thea Guanzon,
The Hurricane Wars

What is **TRUE LOVE.** Is it something that's **DESTINED**? Or is it something that you make? Is it both?

SARAH J. MAAS

Meet me at the corner of
SMUT AVENUE
and
FILTHY STREET

The warm familiarity of the bookshelves kept her together, knit her back into herself as she wandered between them.

Hannah Whitten,
For the Wolf

We crave the magic, the escapism, the real-world analogies... and we want to fall in love while reading them!

Analeigh Sbrana

Mentally, I'm in a cursed library making intense eye contact with a shadow prince

If the world has not **PREPARED** a place for you, you must take up a hammer and chisel and **CARVE** one out for yourself.

A. B. PORANEK,
WHERE THE DARK STANDS STILL

I'M A FIRM BELIEVER THAT WE DO HAVE MAGIC AS HUMANS

THAT COMES THROUGH IN OUR CONNECTIONS WITH OTHERS.

JASON JUNE

Lean in to the tropes

Let's face it, we read romantasy because we love the familiarity and comfort of the storylines, and that inevitably means that some narrative devices crop up time and time again. Instead of trying to avoid clichés, embrace them with glee. "Oh no, there's only one bed"? Excellent. "He's dangerous, but he saved a kitten"? Go wild. "She's the chosen one but doesn't know it yet"? Inject it directly into my veins. Tropes are part of the fun – they're cozy, dramatic, and they bring the vibes. Focus on the joy of the familiar, and the surprise of the subtle twists each author brings to your favourite plot devices.

She was my constant lantern when, like now, the world was dark and I didn't know *which way to go.*

Penn Cole,
Spark of the Everflame

HE'S A TEN BUT
HIS PET IS AN

*elemental
fire beast*

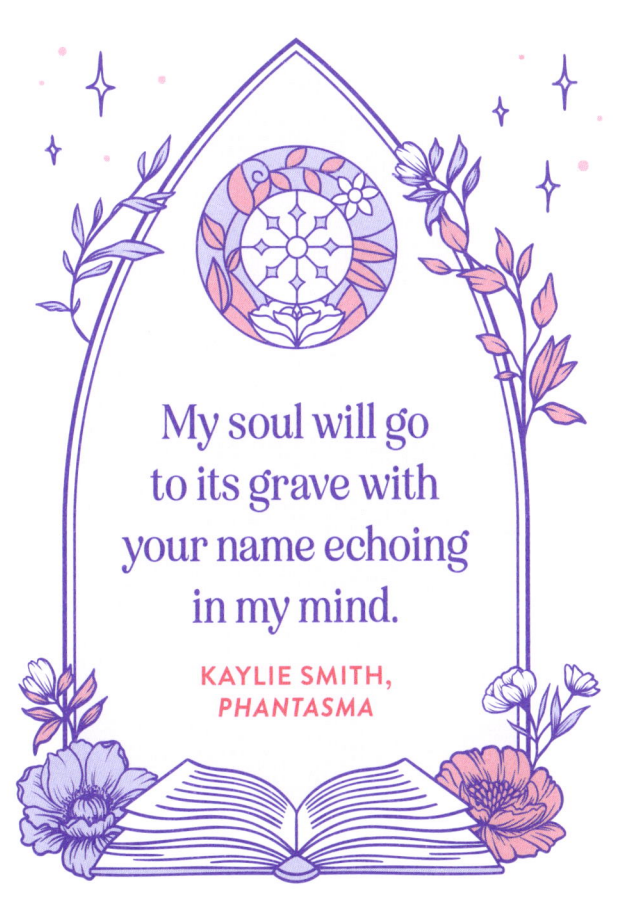

It was like grasping at a flame. I never penetrated to the burning heart of you, only came away with empty, scorched fingers.

S. T. Gibson,
A Dowry of Blood

Never did I imagine such luminous joy existed, and never again would I be content to remain in the shadows.

Sue Lynn Tan,
Daughter of the Moon Goddess

KNEELING BEFORE YOUR SWORN ENEMY IS A LOVE LANGUAGE

I should rather have you than a heap of **GOLD**, even if it were very comfortable to sleep on.

NAOMI NOVIK,
HIS MAJESTY'S DRAGON

The problem with love
is the more you try to destroy
it, the stronger it becomes.
It might look like weakness
on the surface. But in truth,
it's tougher than steel.

KRISTEN CICCARELLI,
REBEL WITCH

Keep a romantasy quote journal

Find a beautiful notebook or journal and use it to write down the most magical quotes and extraordinary moments in each book you read. You could categorize them into love and longing, worldbuilding, epic battles and dragon lore, or just collect together everything that speaks to you and that you want to remember. Take time to write it with calligraphic flourishes, sketches and pressed flowers, or scribble as quickly as you can if you're desperate to get back to the story. The important thing is that you have your own personal grimoire that you can return to whenever you want to soak up your favourite lines.

I don't know who needs to hear this, but your dragon deserves emotional support too

Fantasy – even if something is about to eat you – you're sort of glad it **EXISTS**, because the world is **BIGGER** with it.

HOLLY BLACK

We both embody things that maybe people don't expect to go together, but which surprises them, hopefully in *good ways.*

A. Y. Chao,
Shanghai Immortal

Cloaked in darkness;

BATHED IN FORBIDDEN LOVE

You are the cove of which our storm-struck ships moor. The beacon of light in the darkest night leading us home. A candle whose flame flickers against the coldest wind.

Elizabeth Helen,
Bonded by Thorns

I didn't remember how long we talked, but somewhere amidst her laughter and smiles, I decided I would rip the world apart for her.

Amber V. Nicole,
The Book of Azrael

Sorry,
I can't hear
you over the
sound of my
tragic fate

"Do you love him?" he pressed in an even smaller voice. This time, my smile grew so wide it hurt my cheeks, and my heart fluttered painfully against my chest. "More than anyone has ever loved another, even from before time was made."

GILLIAN ELIZA WEST,
RUIN

SINCE THE MOMENT I SET EYES ON YOU... THERE'S BEEN NO ONE BUT YOU.

EVEN IF I'M A GODDAMNED FOOL FOR IT, THERE WILL NEVER BE ANYONE BUT YOU.

DANIELLE L. JENSEN,
THE BRIDGE KINGDOM

Romantasy playlist

When you can't be reading romantasy (you mean, I have to do housework?), you can still transport yourself to your favourite enchanted realm – through the magic of music. Create playlists for different moods or scenarios that you can put on when you need a burst of escapism – it makes doing the dishes a lot more fun! See what songs you can find that conjure up the feeling of riding into battle with your heart torn in two, or the moment you fall for the dragon prince. Some songs might scream "lonely nights in the castle dungeon", others maybe give "High Queen taking her tea" vibes. Just make sure they're all swoon-tastic.

All of the stars in the sky are not as bright as my *love for you.*

Scarlett St. Clair,
King of Battle and Blood

IT'S GIVING
"I'd burn the realm for you"
ENERGY

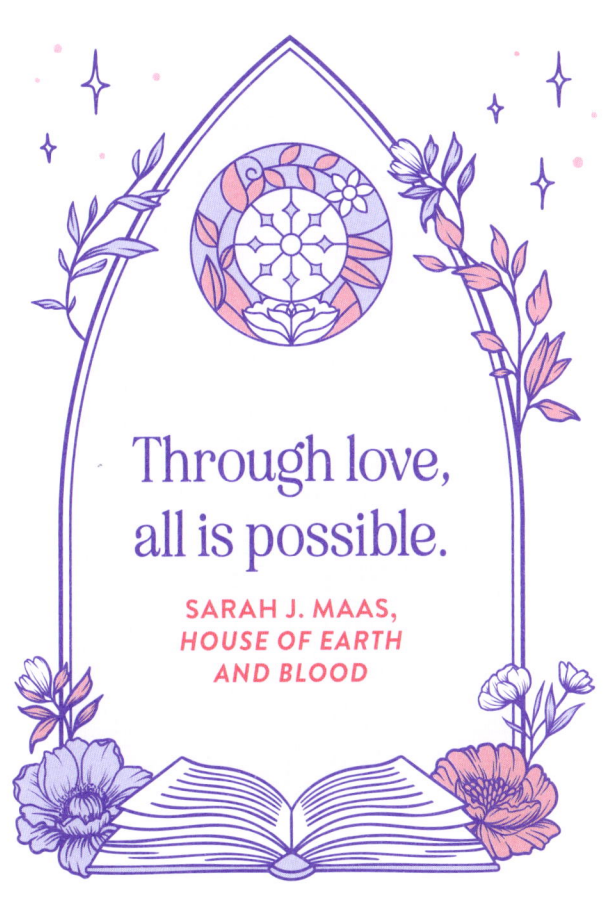

Promise me you won't forget this, Poppy. That no matter what happens tomorrow, the next day, next week, you won't forget this, forget that this was real.

Jennifer L. Armentrout,
From Blood and Ash

It's a leap of faith to love people and let yourself be loved. It's closing your eyes, stepping off a ledge into nothing, and trusting that you'll fly rather than fall.

Sangu Mandanna,
The Very Secret Society of Irregular Witches

IT'S GIVING CURSED SOULMATE ENERGY

THEIR LOVE HAS HUNG ABOVE ME LIKE THE SUN, A BURNING BRIGHTNESS I COULD SURVIVE

ONLY IF I NEVER LOOKED STRAIGHT AT IT, NEVER FLEW TOO CLOSE.

ALIX E. HARROW,
A SPINDLE SPLINTERED

Love is not the sharp-edged thing she's always believed it to be. It's not like the sea, liable to slip through her fingers if she holds on too tight. It's not a currency, something to be earned or denied or bartered for. Love can be steadfast. It can be certain and safe, or as wild as an open flame.

ALLISON SAFT,
A FAR WILDER MAGIC

Illustrate your favourite quote

We all have one: that line that you keep going back to, that makes your heart sing, and that you want tattooed on your heart. It's the line that made you fall in love with that author, and that sums up everything that keeps drawing you back to the world of romantasy. What better way to honour it (in a slightly less permanent way than the tattoo) than to take the time to write it out carefully and beautifully by hand, add some suitably gothic artistic flourishes, and hang it (framed, of course) in your reading nook or gallery wall?

Not me rereading the battle scene just for the way he says, "You're mine."

You cannot be nothing when you are everything to *someone else.*

Lauren Roberts,
Reckless

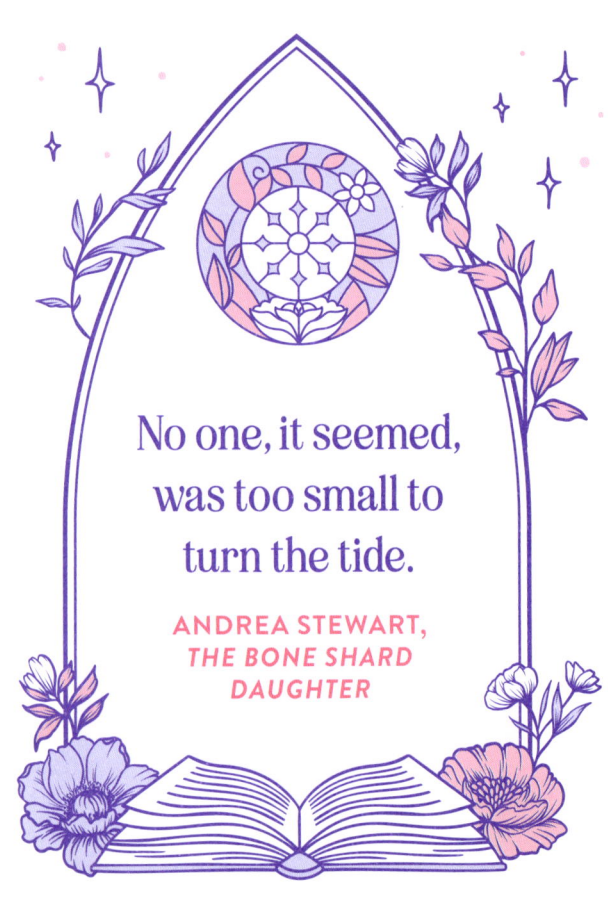

Written in the stars but **CURSED** *by the gods*

Because for now, the world outside didn't exist. There was only her. For the first time in a long time, I felt as if I wasn't lost. I wasn't broken. I was exactly where I was meant to be.

Briar Boleyn,
The Bond That Burns

I give you my body.
I give you my blood.
I give you my soul...
From this night until
the end of nights...
I bind myself to you.

Carissa Broadbent,
The Serpent and the
Wings of Night

I would walk through fire if it led me to you

All stories are made of both **TRUTHS** and **LIES**... What matters is the way that we **BELIEVE** in them.

STEPHANIE GARBER,
ONCE UPON A BROKEN HEART

FOR A MOMENT, HE LOOKED LIKE HE WAS STANDING IN THE NIGHT SKY

AMONG THE STARS, A CONSTELLATION COME TO LIFE.

ANALEIGH SBRANA,
LORE OF THE WILDS

Book swap

One of the joys of being a romantasy fan is that there's just *so much to read*. Even the world's fastest reader would struggle to get through all the brilliant books that feature the tropes and characters we adore. But if you don't have the funds – or the bookshelf space – to buy all the books by your favourite authors, why not host a book swap? Get all your romantasy-loving friends together and ask everyone to bring one book they want back, and one they don't. Everyone gets to go home with a new book for their shelves, as well as a temporary loan of a friend's favourite story. After all, as all fated lovers know, sharing is caring!

I was made of
earth and sky
and endless waters.
I was made to
be loved fully,
or not at all.

Lyra Selene,
A Feather So Black

I'VE BEEN LOOKING FOR YOU SINCE

I heard my first fairytale

A good book was its own brand of magic, one I could safely indulge in without fear of getting caught by those who hunted. I loved escaping from reality, especially during times of trouble. Stories made everything possible.

KERRI MANISCALCO,
KINGDOM OF THE WICKED

To the quiet
girls with stories
in their heads.
To their dreams –
and their nightmares.

Rachel Gillig,
One Dark Window

If you ever find you've **NOWHERE** else to go, you come here to these **BOOKS** and find **YOURSELF.**

J. ELLE,
WINGS OF EBONY

When you finally break the curse and it turns out he was hotter *with* the horns

The intersection of love and magic is a tale as *old as time.*

Thea Guanzon

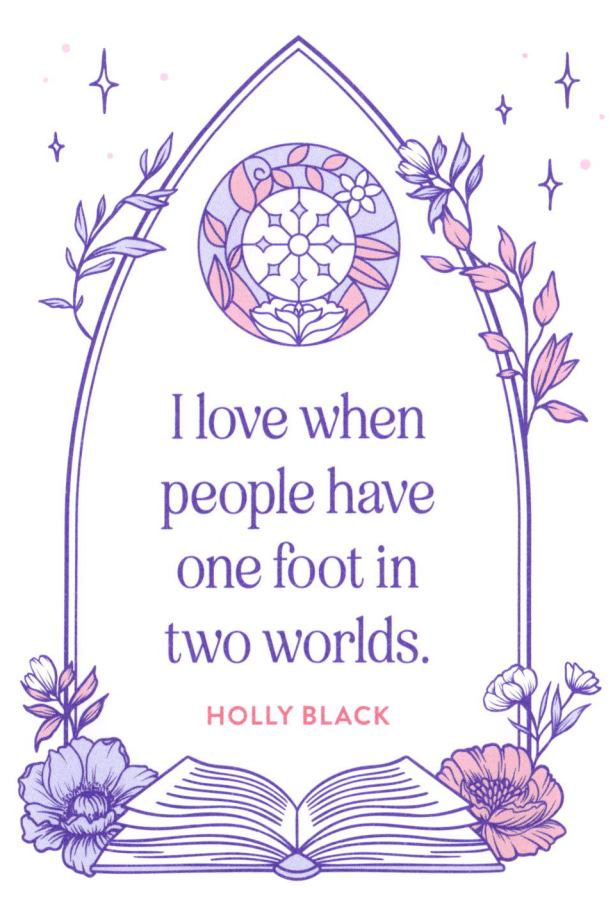

POV:
you just found out your brooding enemy is

YOUR SOULMATE

It's just the ultimate fantasy that someone cares so much about you, they would do anything to make sure you're okay.

Elizabeth Helen

Magic is everywhere... Even humans carry a spark of it in their fragile, fickle souls. All you need to do is reach out and find it.

Heather Walter,
Malice

The joy of rereading

Not all romantasy is created equal, and maybe you just aren't vibing with the new book you only picked up because you couldn't resist that cover. If it's not sweeping you away, it's okay to relegate it to the DNF pile. You deserve magic and pure escapism… and you know that exists, because you've felt it before. It's time to pick up your favourite romantasy novel and sink into the joy of the reread. Let yourself fall into it – and fall for those characters, that banter, that tension, that world – all over again. The reread is powerful because it gives us comfort and safety, and most of all, it brings back the magic.

You're my favourite kind of plot twist

To the women who **REWRITE** the rules, one page at a time. Your potential is the plot twist the world never saw coming.

HELEN SCHEUERER,
IRON & EMBERS

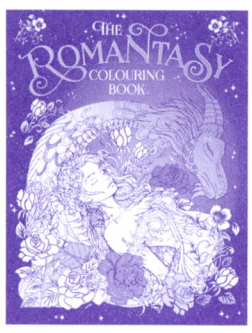

The Romantasy Colouring Book: A Fantastical Journey of Colour and Creativity

Paperback

ISBN: 978-1-83799-604-9

The Romantasy Puzzle Book: 200 Brain-Teasing Activities Inspired by Magical Realms, Faraway Kingdoms and Enchanting Romances

Francis Nightingale

Hardback

ISBN: 978-1-83799-684-1

The Romantasy Cocktail Book: 52 Enchanting Recipes to Spice up Your Night

Francis Nightingale

Hardback

ISBN: 978-1-83799-730-5

You Had Me at Dragons: Smouldering Quotes and Passionate Affirmations for Romantasy Fans

Hardback

ISBN: 978-1-83799-932-3

Have you enjoyed this book?

If so, find us on Facebook at **Summersdale Publishers**, on Twitter/X at **@Summersdale** and on Instagram, TikTok and Bluesky at **@summersdalebooks** and get in touch. We'd love to hear from you!

www.summersdale.com

IMAGE CREDITS

Cover and throughout: Book and stars © kichikimi/Shutterstock.com; Stained glass © Rizka Silvia/Shutterstock.com; Flowers © Feodora_21/Shutterstock.com; Window frame © PavloArt Studio/Shutterstock.com
Insides only: Chunky stars © Oleksandra Klestova/Shutterstock.com; Dagger, small crystal and arrow © Oleksandra Klestova/Shutterstock.com; Dragon © Oleksandra Klestova/Shutterstock.com; Large crystal © lavendertime/Shutterstock.com; Moon phase illustration © Svetlana Avv/Shutterstock.com; Rose © IgorijArt/Shutterstock.com; Scattered star motif © Tamiris6/Shutterstock.com; Sparkle motif © kichikimi/Shutterstock.com